First published in Great Britain in hardback in 2001 by Brimax
First paperback edition published in Great Britain in 2002 by Brimax
An imprint of Octopus Publishing Group Ltd
2-4 Heron Quays, London E14 4JP
© Octopus Publishing Group Ltd

ISBN 1 85854 307 X (hardback)
ISBN 1 85854 496 3 (paperback)

Printed in Italy

Tiny's Big Wish

BRIMAX

In Africa, where the grass
grows high and the ostriches stretch
their necks to see across the plains,
the elephants are marching.

"Hup, two, three, four!
We elephants are very sure:
Sure that we are big and strong,
With enormous ears and trunks so long.
We're always brave, we're always bold...
We're always warm and never cold!
Hup, two, three, four!
Who could ask for anything more?"

On and on the elephants march,
down to the river to drink. But not all of
the elephants are big and strong. Not all
of them are brave and bold. There is one
elephant who is very small.
He has little baby legs that cannot march
quickly enough, so he is always
running behind the others.

This is Tiny.

Tiny trips over his little elephant feet.
Then he trips over his little elephant trunk.
His mother waits for him to catch her up
and takes him down to the river.

"Oh dear," sighs Tiny as his
mother scrubs his back.
"I wish I was big. I wish I was strong.
I wish I was brave. And I wish
I could march in time."

Then Tiny sings his own sad, little song:

"Little is such a hard thing to be,
Everyone else is bigger than me.
I wish I was brave,
I wish I was strong,
I wish my trunk was ever so long!
I wish I could march:
Hup, two, three, four,
And not be a baby anymore."

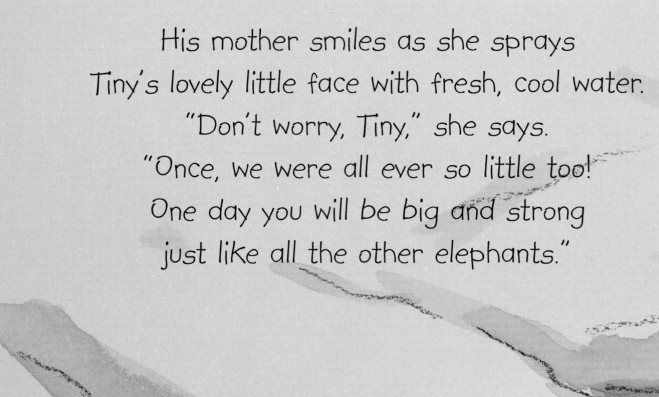

His mother smiles as she sprays
Tiny's lovely little face with fresh, cool water.
"Don't worry, Tiny," she says.
"Once, we were all ever so little too!
One day you will be big and strong
just like all the other elephants."

Tiny looks up at his mother.
He looks up from her big, wrinkly
knees to her big, crinkly ears; from her
bright, blinking eyes to the top of her
great, domed head.

"As big as you?" he asks.
"Bigger!" says his mother.

But Tiny wanders off shaking
his head sadly, because he doesn't
quite believe her.

"I wish I was big and had an enormous great body just like you!" says Tiny to the old water buffalo.
"Don't worry, Tiny," says Buffalo.
"One day your body will be enormous too."
Tiny looks up at him.
He looks up from Buffalo's great long mane to his curled long horns, right to the top of his great hairy head.
"As big as yours?" he asks.
"Bigger!" says Buffalo
But Tiny wanders off shaking his head sadly. He doesn't quite believe it!

"I wish I was big and had a gigantic great belly just like you!" says Tiny to Harry the hippo.
"Don't worry, Tiny," says Harry.
"One day your belly will be enormous too."
Tiny looks up at him. He looks up from Harry's huge feet to his great, yawning mouth, to the top of Harry's enormous flat head. "As big as yours?" he asks.
"Bigger!" says Harry.
But still Tiny does not quite believe him!

He decides to ask some of the other animals.
Will I be as tall as you one day?"
Tiny asks Ostrich.
"Taller!" says Ostrich.
"Hmm!" says Tiny, thinking hard,

"Will I be bigger than you one day?"
Tiny asks Zebra.
"Of course!" says Zebra, laughing.
"Will I really be big and tall one day?"
Tiny asks the lions and scampering warthogs.
"Of course!" they all say, and smile
at the little elephant.

Tiny goes back to the herd, who are all busy munching and chomping to keep themselves big and strong. Finally Tiny believes what he has been told.

"I will be bigger than you one day,"
Tiny tells his mother.
"I will be stronger than you one day,"
Tiny tells his big sister.
"I'll have a longer trunk than you one day,"
Tiny tells his aunt.
"We know" they all laugh together.

This time, as the herd marches off, Tiny
stomps along proudly beside his mother,
and he sings his new song .

"Being so little is not so bad,
It's not for ever, so I won't be sad.
I will be brave, I will be strong,
I will have a trunk that's ever so long!
I'll march in time:
Hup, two, three, four,
And not be the baby anymore."

And now, all the elephants agree, Tiny will be
the biggest, bravest elephant of them all!

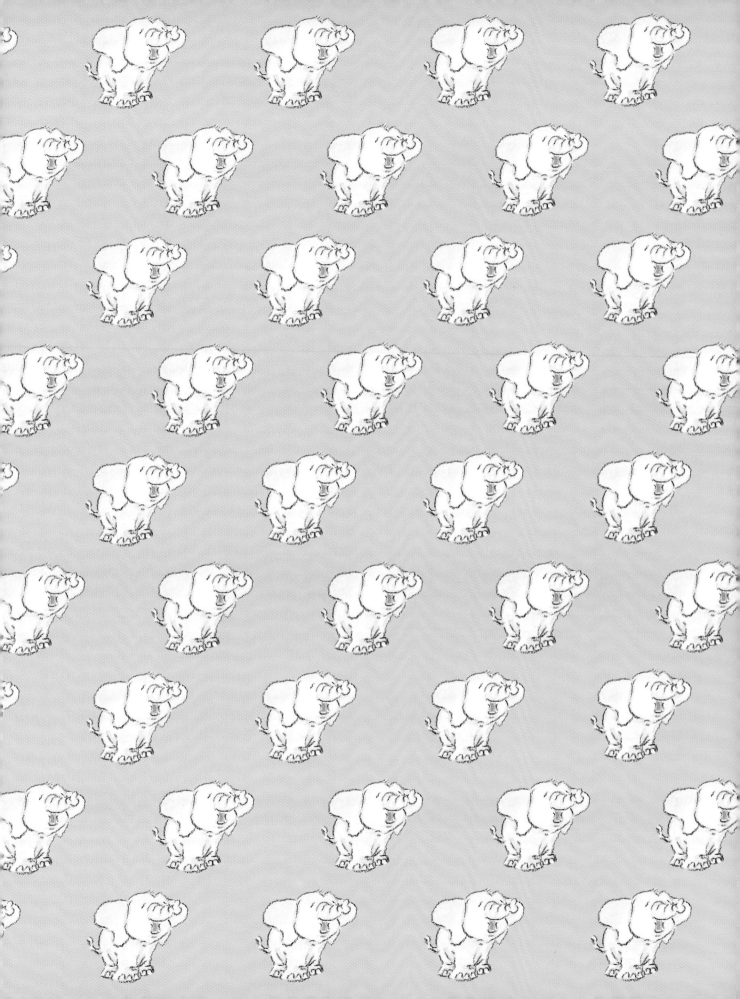